Illustrated by Tessa Carlson
Cover photo illustration by Tessa Carlson
Edited by Lily Coyle and Hanna Kjeldbjerg
Managing editor: Hanna Kjeldbjerg

ISBN 13: 978-1-59298-816-7
Library of Congress Catalog Number: 2018913702
Printed in the United States of America
First Printing: 2019
23 22 21 20 19   5 4 3 2 1

Book design and typesetting by Dan Pitts.

BEAVER'S POND
PRESS

Beaver's Pond Press
7108 Ohms Lane
Edina, MN 55439–2129
(952) 829-8818
www.BeaversPondPress.com

To order, visit www.ItascaBooks.com
or call (952) 345-4488.
Reseller discounts available.

Contact Pamela Fish Carlson at
www.EmmaBeeBook.com for speaking
engagements, book club discussions,
freelance writing projects,
and interviews.

Emma Bee

Story by
**Pamela
Fish Carlson**

Illustrated by
Tessa Carlson

Beaver's Pond
PRESS

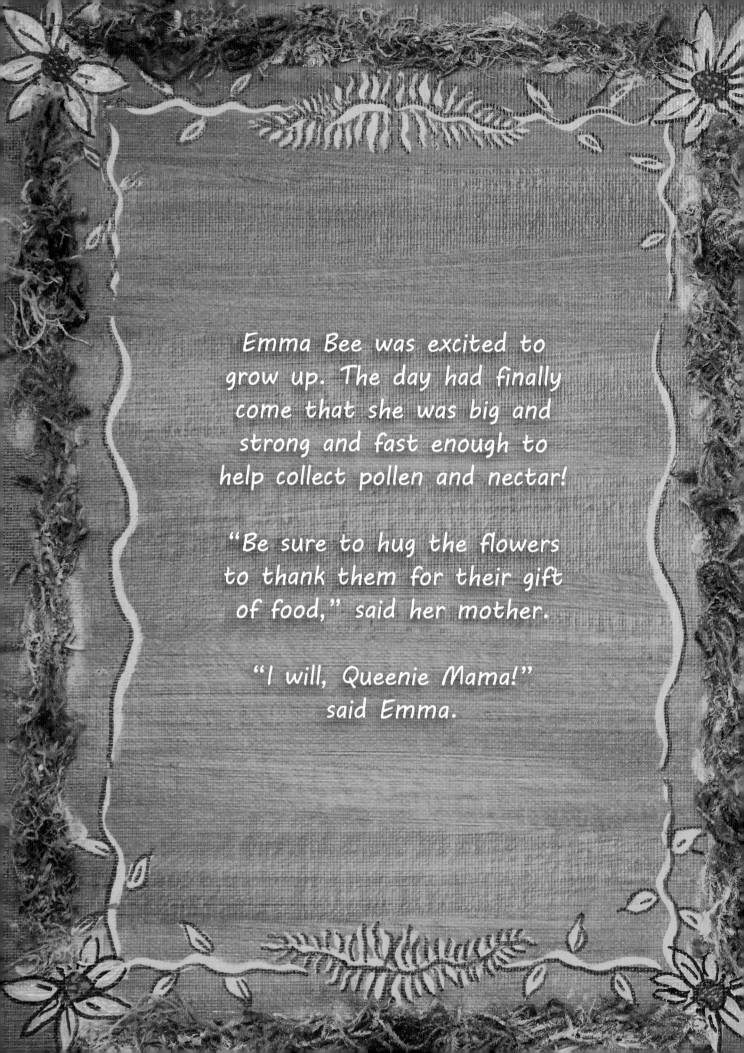

Emma Bee was excited to grow up. The day had finally come that she was big and strong and fast enough to help collect pollen and nectar!

"Be sure to hug the flowers to thank them for their gift of food," said her mother.

"I will, Queenie Mama!" said Emma.

"And stay out of Mrs. Muggin's
yard. You can tell where
Mrs. Muggin lives because
the flowers are straight
and tall and all look the same,"
warned her mother.

Emma agreed and
happily buzzed away.

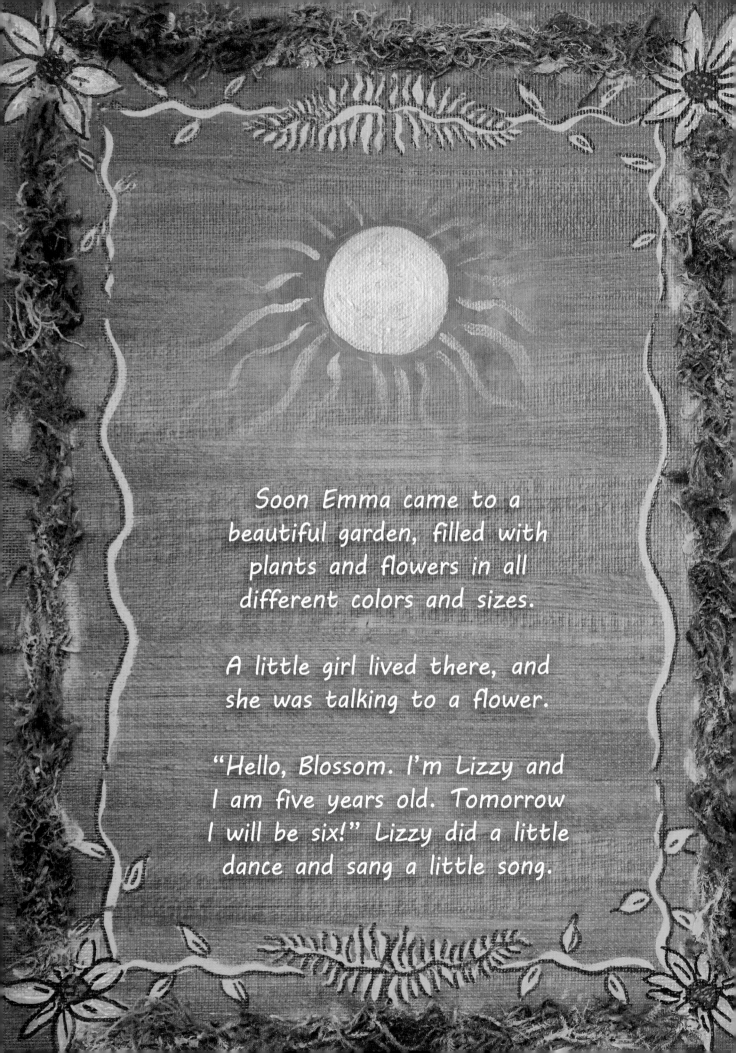

Soon Emma came to a
beautiful garden, filled with
plants and flowers in all
different colors and sizes.

A little girl lived there, and
she was talking to a flower.

"Hello, Blossom. I'm Lizzy and
I am five years old. Tomorrow
I will be six!" Lizzy did a little
dance and sang a little song.

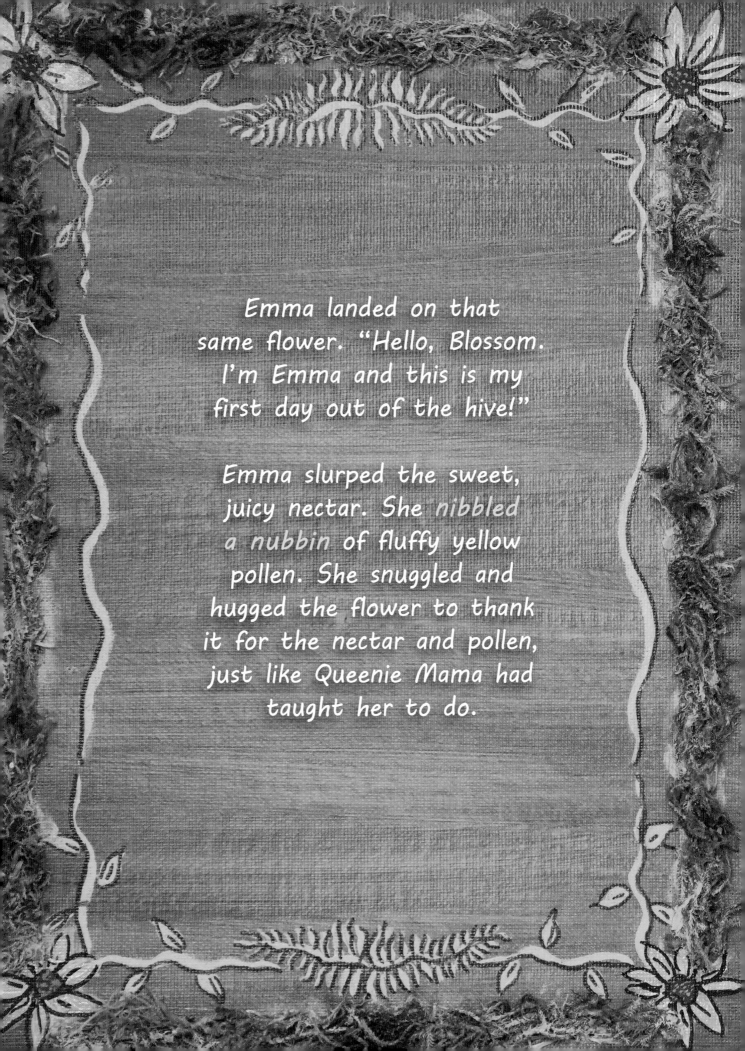

Emma landed on that
same flower. "Hello, Blossom.
I'm Emma and this is my
first day out of the hive!"

Emma slurped the sweet,
juicy nectar. She nibbled
a nubbin of fluffy yellow
pollen. She snuggled and
hugged the flower to thank
it for the nectar and pollen,
just like Queenie Mama had
taught her to do.

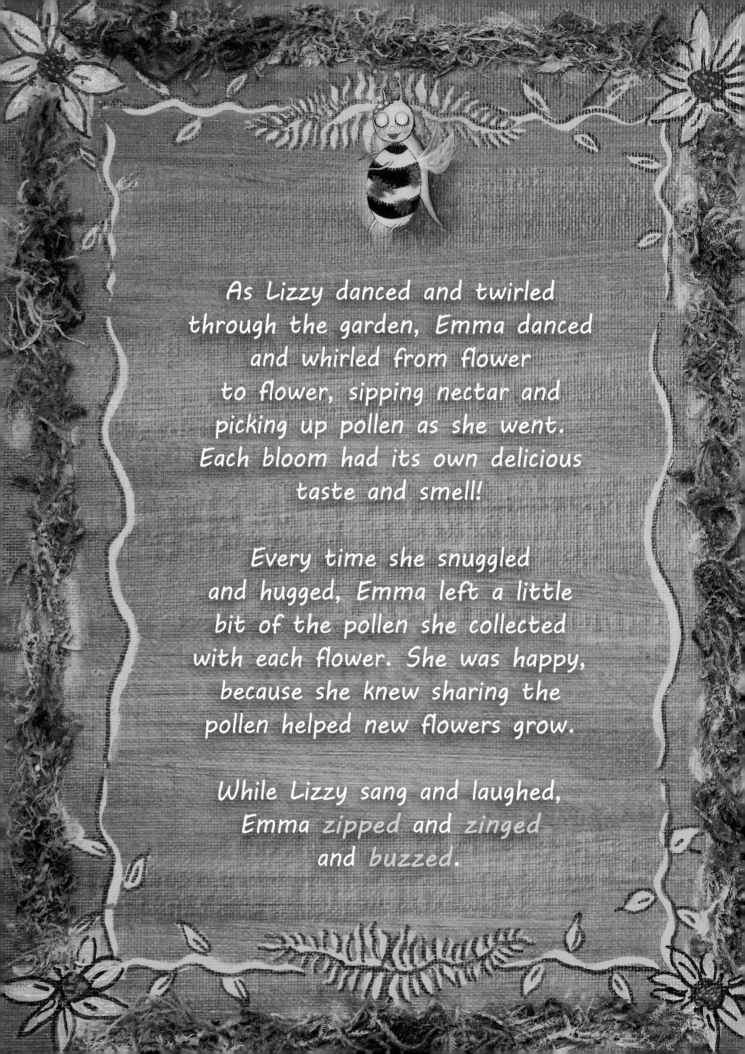

As Lizzy danced and twirled
through the garden, Emma danced
and whirled from flower
to flower, sipping nectar and
picking up pollen as she went.
Each bloom had its own delicious
taste and smell!

Every time she snuggled
and hugged, Emma left a little
bit of the pollen she collected
with each flower. She was happy,
because she knew sharing the
pollen helped new flowers grow.

While Lizzy sang and laughed,
Emma *zipped* and *zinged*
and *buzzed*.

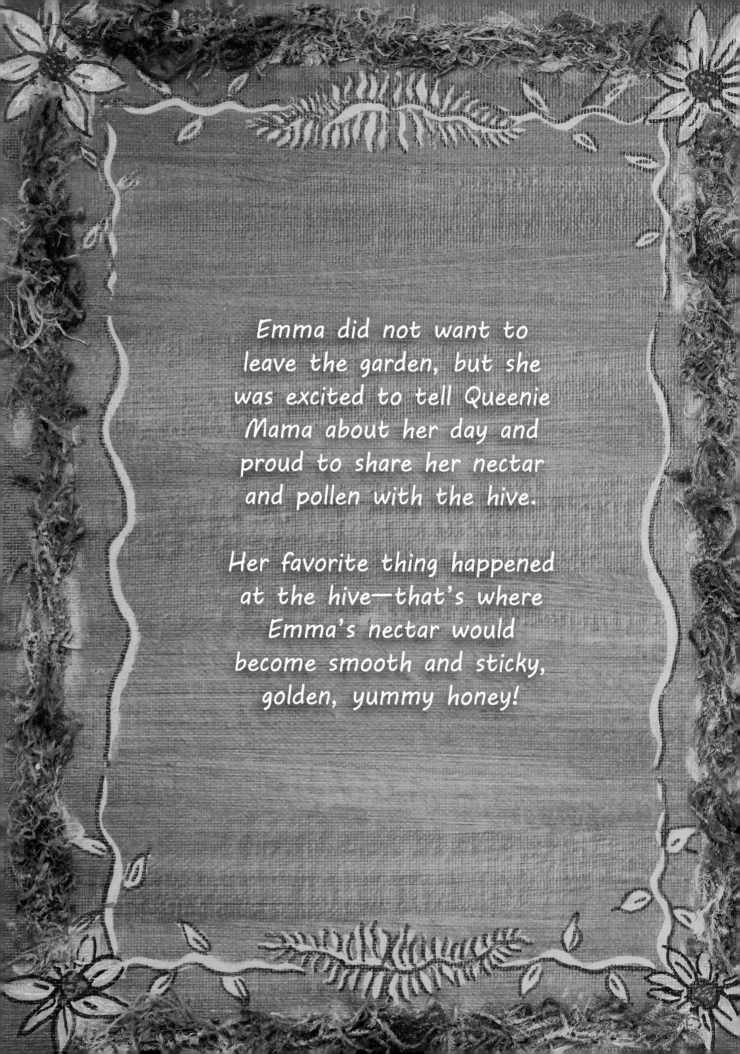

Emma did not want to
leave the garden, but she
was excited to tell Queenie
Mama about her day and
proud to share her nectar
and pollen with the hive.

Her favorite thing happened
at the hive—that's where
Emma's nectar would
become smooth and sticky,
golden, yummy honey!

The next day, Emma
made a beeline back to
the beautiful garden.

When she got there,
Emma saw several
children playing among
the flowers. Lizzy was
having a birthday party!

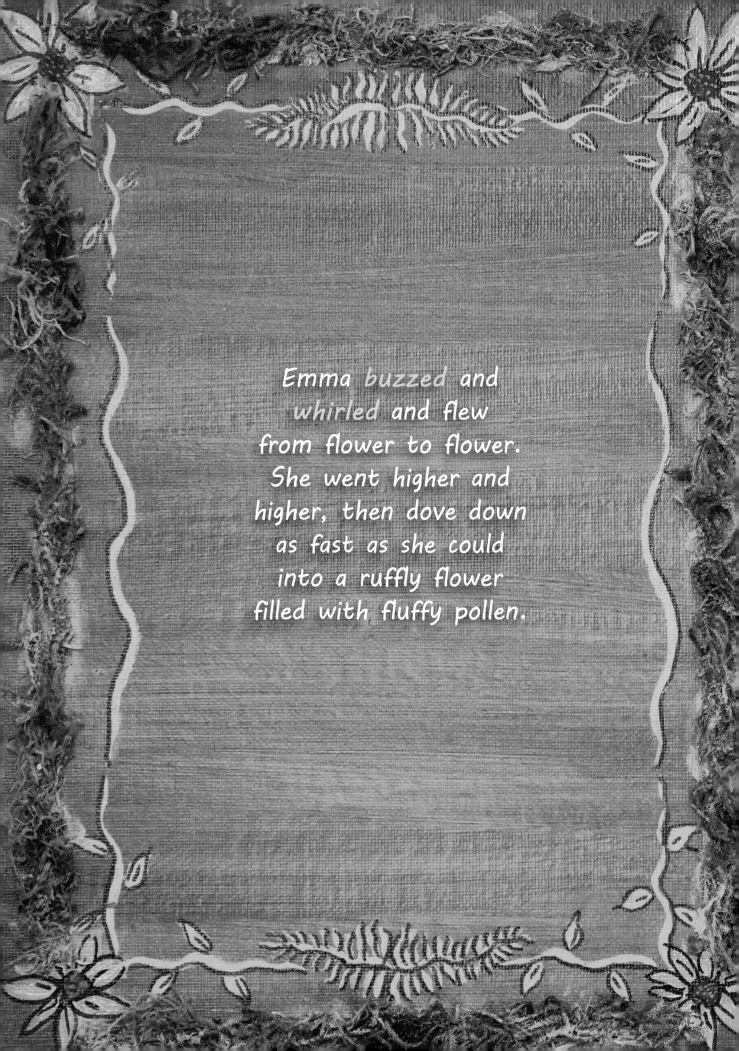

Emma buzzed and
whirled and flew
from flower to flower.
She went higher and
higher, then dove down
as fast as she could
into a ruffly flower
filled with fluffy pollen.

Suddenly, one of the children
yelled, "Bee! Bee! Watch out!
It's going to sting you!"

Emma didn't understand.
Bees use their stingers only when
they're in danger, and she was
having fun at Lizzy's party!
Why would she sting them?

Zipping and zinging, she tried
to make the children like her by
showing off some of her best
flying tricks. But that just made
the children scream and run
and flap their arms.

Emma worried they might
swat her. Even Lizzy looked sad
and a little bit frightened.

So Emma left Lizzy, the party,
and the beautiful garden. She was
so unhappy, she could hardly buzz.

As she flew by the straight
and tall flowers that
all looked the same,
she remembered she
couldn't go home
without nectar and
pollen. The flowers were
all in neat rows, so it
would be easy to zip
and zing from flower
to flower here.

Emma didn't see
Mrs. Muggin nearby, so in she went.
Emma thought she was big and
strong and fast enough to get
in and out in a jiffy.

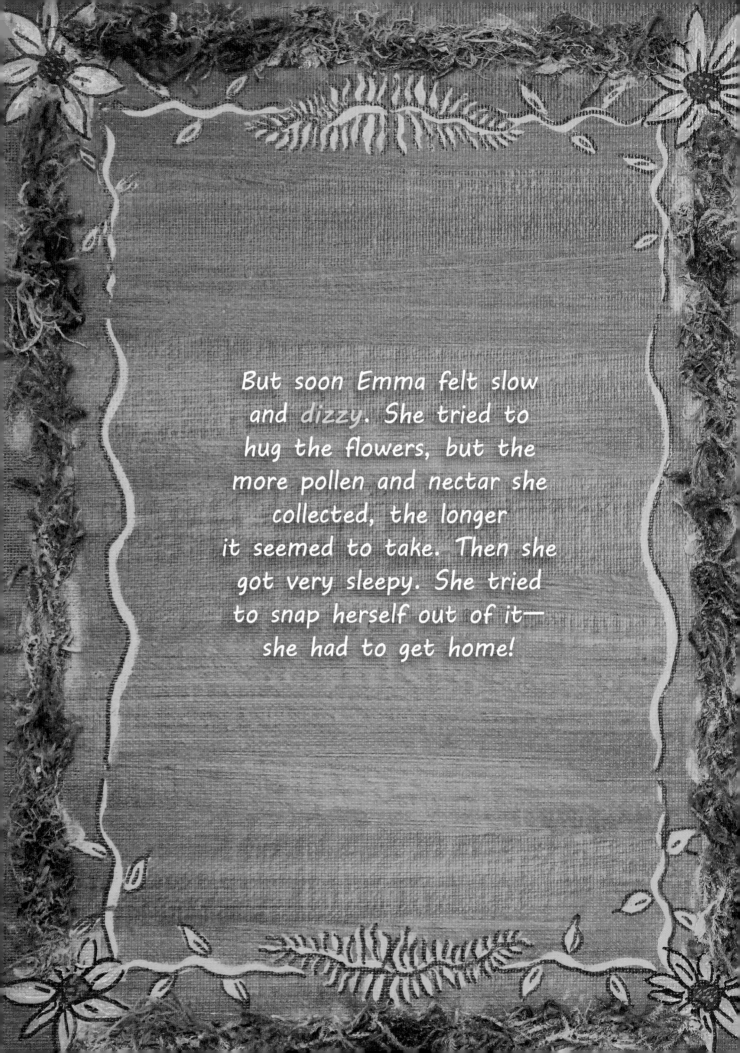

But soon Emma felt slow
and *dizzy*. She tried to
hug the flowers, but the
more pollen and nectar she
collected, the longer
it seemed to take. Then she
got very sleepy. She tried
to snap herself out of it—
she had to get home!

It took a very long time,
but somehow she made it
back to the hive.

Emma's mother was happy to
see her, but sad to
learn what happened.
"Now you know about
Mrs. Muggin's yard,"
said Queenie Mama.
"She sprays a stinky foggy
potion on her flowers to make
them look just right, and that
potion makes
bees sick."

The next day Emma felt well
enough to gather more pollen
and nectar. She quickly passed
by Mrs. Muggin's yard.

Before she knew it, she was
back at the edge of the
beautiful garden.

Emma hid behind a branch
and spied, unsure if she
should go in.

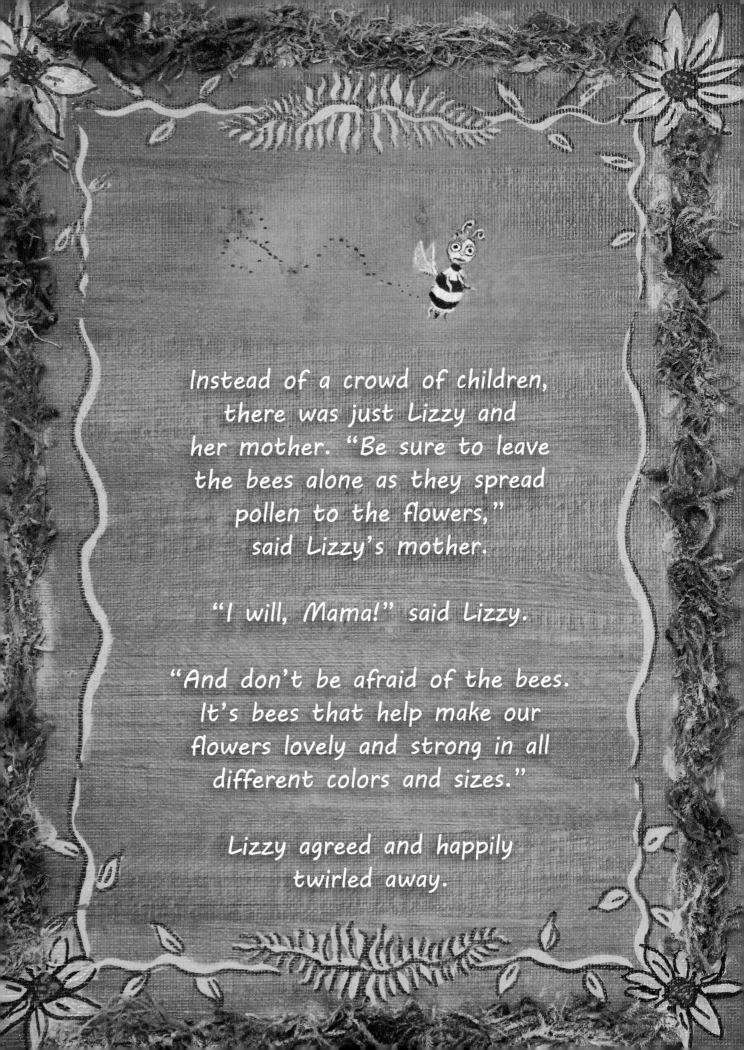

Instead of a crowd of children,
there was just Lizzy and
her mother. "Be sure to leave
the bees alone as they spread
pollen to the flowers,"
said Lizzy's mother.

"I will, Mama!" said Lizzy.

"And don't be afraid of the bees.
It's bees that help make our
flowers lovely and strong in all
different colors and sizes."

Lizzy agreed and happily
twirled away.

How glad this made Emma!

As Lizzy danced and twirled
through the garden, Emma danced
and whirled from flower to
flower, and gave each flower
a snuggle and a hug. Lizzy sang
and laughed, and Emma zipped
and zinged and buzzed until it
was time to go home.

Lizzy was so thankful for all the
plants and flowers. And Emma
was so happy to be a honeybee!

Did You Know?

70 percent of all flowering plants are pollinated by bees, insects, and other animals.

One out of every three bites of food depends on bees and other animals for pollination.

Honeybees will attack only when they feel threatened.

The United States is in a honeybee crisis— huge numbers of honeybee hives have been lost in the last several years, largely due to pesticides and habitat loss.

Four Ways to Help Bees

1. Plant bee flowers everywhere.
2. Keep bee flowers clean—don't use pesticides.
3. YouTube "how to make a bee home" with your parent or guardian.
4. Spread the word about how honeybees are friendly and need to be protected!

For more information on bees, visit www.EmmaBeeBook.com with a parent or guardian.

Plant a Flower, Save a Bee

Try these!

Bluebell

Lavender

Sunflower

Goldenrod

Chive

Poppy

Lupine

Black-Eyed Susan